Special thanks to
Sarah Levison

ORCHARD BOOKS
Carmelite House
50 Victoria Embankment
London EC4Y 0DZ

First published in Great Britain in 2016
This Happy Reader edition published for McDonald's in 2017
by The Watts Publishing Group.

A CIP catalogue record for this book is available
from the British Library.

ISBN 978 1 40835 191 8

1 3 5 7 9 10 8 6 4 2

Printed in Slovakia

Orchard Books
An imprint of Hachette Children's Group
Part of The Watts Publishing Group Limited
An Hachette UK Company
www.hachette.co.uk

MIX
Paper from
responsible sources
FSC® C104740

The paper and board used in this book are made from wood
from responsible sources.

Twilight Sparkle's Princess Spell

ORCHARD

Princess Celestia
is the ruler of all
Equestria! She is
beautiful, kind
and wise. Her
cutie mark is
a sun.

Twilight
Sparkle is
learning all
about magic.
Her cutie
mark is a
pink star.

Rainbow Dash
is a fast Pegasus
pony. She helps
to control the
weather. Her
cutie mark is
a cloud with
a rainbow
lightning bolt.

Spike the dragon is
Twilight Sparkle's
assistant.

Rarity is a glamorous unicorn. Her cutie mark is three blue diamonds.

Fluttershy is very quiet and shy. She loves animals. Her cutie mark is three pink butterflies.

Pinkie Pie loves to have fun and make people laugh. Her cutie mark is three bouncing balloons!

Applejack works on a farm. Her cutie mark is three red apples.

Contents

PART ONE
Cutie Mark Chaos 12

PART TWO
The Friendship Fix 30

PART THREE
The Princess Spell 50

PART ONE
Cutie Mark Chaos

Chapter One

A Very Special Delivery

One day, when Twilight
Sparkle got home after a lovely
day, she heard a knock at the
door. It was a delivery pony.
He had a special package
for Twilight Sparkle, from
Princess Celestia!

There was a note with it. In the note, Princess Celestia told Twilight Sparkle about a strange spell she had found.

Twilight read the magic spell out loud:

From one to another, another to one. A magical mix-up has just begun!

"That doesn't make any sense," Twilight Sparkle said to her dragon assistant, Spike.

Putting down the note, Twilight decided she would look at the spell later.

Twilight Sparkle trotted into Ponyville. There were lots of ponies everywhere and Twilight was feeling happy.

Then, suddenly, a huge burst of rainwater hit her, soaking her from mane to tail!

"Rainbow Dash! That's NOT funny!" Twilight cried.

Rainbow Dash looked after the weather in Ponyville.

Twilight thought that Rainbow Dash had made it rain on her on purpose as a joke.

But the pony controlling the raincloud wasn't Rainbow Dash. It was Rarity!

Chapter Two

Friends in Trouble

"Sorry, darling!" Rarity said.

Rarity had a shop in Ponyville. Twilight Sparkle wondered why Rarity was trying to control the weather instead of Rainbow Dash. She wasn't doing a very good job!

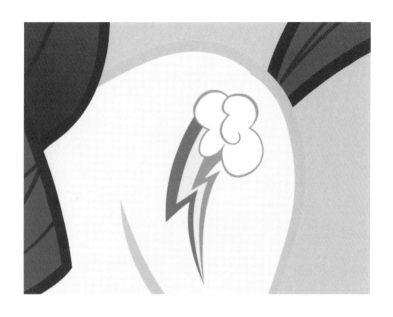

Just then, Twilight Sparkle noticed something on Rarity's side. She had Rainbow Dash's cutie mark!

A cutie mark was a very special picture that adult ponies had on their back leg.

A cutie mark showed the pony's special talent. Rainbow Dash's cutie mark was a cloud with a rainbow lightning bolt.

Twilight Sparkle knew that ponies shouldn't be able to swap cutie marks! What was going on? She tried to ask Rarity, but her friend was too busy trying to sort out the weather mess.

Twilight decided to ask her friend Fluttershy what was happening. Fluttershy lived in a cottage with lots of animals.

But when Twilight Sparkle reached the cottage, it was her friend Rainbow Dash who answered the door.

"Rainbow Dash, what's going on?" asked Twilight Sparkle. The little cottage was in a big mess!

Fluttershy's special talent was helping animals … but she wasn't there, and all of the animals were fighting with each other!

"They don't listen to me!" Rainbow Dash told Twilight Sparkle sadly.

As she turned around, Twilight Sparkle noticed that Rainbow Dash had Fluttershy's cutie mark on her leg!

Twilight Sparkle knew that each of her friends had a special talent. But somehow, all their talents seemed to have been mixed up! Twilight decided to call her dragon assistant, Spike. They had to find out what was going on!

Chapter Three

Magical Mix-ups

The next stop was Sugarcube
Corner, the cake shop where
Pinkie Pie worked. Pinkie Pie
was always full of fun and
energy. But she wasn't there.
The pony trying to look after
the shop was Fluttershy!

She was very unhappy. Twilight Sparkle checked Fluttershy's leg. There was Pinkie Pie's bright balloon cutie mark.

Twilight Sparkle and Spike quickly headed to Sweet Apple Acres, Applejack's home. There they saw poor Pinkie Pie struggling with Applejack's farm chores. She couldn't do any farm work. On her side was Applejack's cutie mark, three red apples.

Twilight Sparkle and Spike had one last place to visit.

The Carousel Boutique was Rarity's shop. It should have been full of beautiful dresses. But today, poor Applejack was struggling with the sewing machine. And she had Rarity's cutie mark!

All Twilight Sparkle's friends had their talents mixed up!

"This is very bad!" Twilight cried. Just then, she remembered Princess Celestia's note.

"It must have been that strange spell!" she told Spike. "It's made my friends forget what their own special talents are. I've got to find a way to make things right."

Ponyville was in big trouble. The weather was snowy, too rainy and too hot. No apples grew on the trees.

Worse of all, all the ponies were fighting with each other. It was a disaster! Twilight Sparkle had to find a way to fix things!

PART TWO
The Friendship Fix

Chapter One

A Pony Plan!

Spike the dragon tried to cheer up his best friend, Twilight Sparkle.

"You'll figure out a way to make things better," said the kind dragon. "After all, these are your friends!"

Twilight Sparkle thought about what Spike had said. He was right. Rainbow Dash, Rarity, Fluttershy, Pinkie Pie and Applejack were her best friends in the whole world!

As Twilight Sparkle thought about her friends, she noticed her magical tiara was starting to glow! Her tiara was kept in a special glass case and it had a magical jewel in the middle of it. Each of her friends had magic jewels too, but theirs were in pretty necklaces.

Twilight Sparkle realised what she needed to do.

"I've got it!" she cried. "I need to help my friends remember what their special talents are!"

Twilight Sparkle put on her crown and rushed out the door.

Spike followed her, carrying the five necklaces.

First, Twilight Sparkle found her friend Fluttershy.

"Fluttershy, will you help Rainbow Dash?" asked Twilight Sparkle. "She's trying to look after all of her animal friends."

Fluttershy looked worried. "But, Twilight, I don't know anything about animals …" she said shyly.

Twilight Sparkle gasped in amazement.

Normally Fluttershy knew more about animals than anyone! Twilight knew she had to make her friend remember her special talent.

"Please Fluttershy, we really need to help Rainbow Dash!" pleaded Twilight Sparkle.

Kind Fluttershy agreed to help Rainbow Dash. The two ponies galloped to the cottage. But as they got closer, they heard horrible squeaks and squawks coming from inside!

Chapter Two

Rainbow Dash Rescue

Fluttershy and Twilight Sparkle opened the door. Inside, all the animals were making a terrible, loud noise.

Twilight Sparkle was worried. Would Fluttershy be brave enough to talk to the animals?

If Fluttershy helped the animals, she might remember her special talent. Then, when she was her normal self again, maybe her butterfly cutie mark would return.

Fluttershy took a deep breath and then called softly to the animals. "Hello, little woodland creatures! Would you like a nice snack?"

As the kind pony offered greens, acorns and birdseed to the animals, they became peaceful and friendly.

Angel Bunny leaped into
Fluttershy's arms for a cuddle
and a bear gave them both a
hug! A bright glow surrounded
Fluttershy. Then, suddenly, her
beautiful butterfly cutie marks
returned! The magical necklace
appeared on Fluttershy's neck.

Twilight Sparkle was so pleased that her plan had worked. Fluttershy had her cutie mark back!

"Come on, Fluttershy!" Twilight Sparkle said. "We need to help the rest of our friends."

Next they went to see Rarity. She still hadn't learned to control the weather. Fluttershy and Twilight Sparkle asked Rainbow Dash if she would fly around and move the clouds for Rarity.

Rainbow Dash wasn't sure at first, but as soon as she zoomed through the skies, she felt much better! Rainbow Dash quickly fixed the weather muddle and her thundercloud and lightning cutie mark magically came back.

Twilight Sparkle was so happy to see Fluttershy and Rainbow Dash back to normal. Next they needed to help Rarity and Applejack, and that meant a visit to the Carousel Boutique.

Chapter Three
Friends Forever

The four pony friends cantered to the Carousel Boutique. Rarity was going to help poor Applejack. Although the farm pony was trying her very best, she just didn't have Rarity's flair for fashion!

Rarity used her magical unicorn horn to put things right. Soon Rarity's cutie mark was back to normal.

"What a terrible dream!" she exclaimed, looking down at the beautiful necklace sparkling around her neck.

There was no time for Twilight Sparkle to explain what had really happened. They needed to pay a visit to Sweet Apple Acres so that Applejack could help Pinkie Pie on the farm.

At the farm, all the friends worked together. They planted new seeds, fixed a broken water pipe and collected lots of delicious apples.

As everyone worked to fix the farm, Applejack's special apple cutie marks returned to her side, and her necklace suddenly appeared around her neck. The farm pony had her special talent back!

"Yee hah!" Applejack cheered. "Who do we need to help next?"

"The townspeople are furious. We need Pinkie Pie to make them happy and full of fun again!" cried Twilight.

Pinkie Pie was normally the most cheerful pony in Ponyville. But when the friends found her, she was so gloomy

that even her bouncy, pink
mane was flat and sad.

Applejack gave Pinkie Pie
a funny costume to wear.
Soon Pinkie Pie was making
everyone laugh and smile.

Twilight Sparkle gave a huge
sigh of relief as Pinkie Pie's

cutie mark returned to normal and the necklace shone around her neck. By working together and being true friends, the ponies had managed to clear up the cutie mark confusion!

PART THREE
The Princess Spell

Chapter One

Wonderful Wings

Helping her friends had shown Twilight Sparkle what to do with Princess Celestia's spell. If she changed it, there would never be cutie mark confusion ever again! Twilight Sparkle returned home.

With her friends' help, she thought of some different words for the spell:

"From all of us together, Working with our friends, A mix-up we'll fix-up, Friendship magic never ends!"

Light shone from the necklaces worn by Rainbow Dash, Fluttershy, Rarity, Pinkie Pie and Applejack, and a beautiful light surrounded Twilight

Sparkle. With an enormous flash, she disappeared!

Twilight Sparkle found herself floating high in the sky, surrounded by stars and a swirling mist. "What is this place?" she said.

Just then, a beautiful pony appeared through the mist … it was Princess Celestia!

"Congratulations, Twilight!" smiled the princess. "I knew you could do it!"

"What did I do?" asked Twilight Sparkle in amazement.

Princess Celestia smiled and
shook her rainbow-coloured
mane. "You used the magic of
friendship to fix an old spell.
You've proven that you are
ready, Twilight!"

Moments later, a bright,
star-shaped light surrounded
Twilight Sparkle. The magical

light carried Twilight back
down to Ponyville, where her
friends were waiting.

"Twilight Sparkle, is that
you?" asked Applejack.

As the light faded the friends
saw that it *was* Twilight Sparkle
… but now she had
a pair of beautiful wings on
her back!

Chapter Two

Castle Coronation

"Awesome! A new flying buddy!" cried Rainbow Dash, rushing forwards to hug Twilight Sparkle.

"Woo hoo!" yelled Pinkie Pie, jumping up and down and waving balloons.

"Wow, you look just like a princess!" breathed Fluttershy.

"That's because she IS a princess." replied Princess Celestia as she appeared behind Twilight Sparkle.

All the ponies were shocked, but Twilight Sparkle was more shocked than anyone!

"You are now Princess Twilight Sparkle," said Princess Celestia with a smile. "By fixing the spell, you've shown that you have what it takes to be a true princess."

Twilight Sparkle's friends bowed down in front of Ponyville's newest princess!

That night, the ponies went to Canterlot Castle for a very special party. Rainbow Dash, Pinkie Pie, Rarity, Applejack, Fluttershy and Spike all joined Princess Celestia and Princess

Luna on stage by the royal thrones. Everyone wore their finest dresses and hats and Spike wore a smart jacket and bow tie.

"Twilight Sparkle has done many amazing things," Princess Celestia said. "So she has become a princess! Everyone please welcome Princess Twilight Sparkle!"

Chapter Three

Princess in Ponyville

The ponies all stamped their
hooves and cheered as Princess
Twilight Sparkle came into
the throne room. She wore a
beautiful pink and gold dress
and was followed by pretty
white ponies.

Spike presented Twilight Sparkle with a glittering crown. Twilight Sparkle smiled at her friends. She still couldn't believe she was a princess!

Princess Twilight Sparkle, Princess Celestia and Princess Luna went out onto the balcony. They waved to the huge crowd gathered below in the castle courtyard.

"Say something, Princess," said Princess Celestia.

Princess Twilight Sparkle suddenly felt very shy!

Turning around, she saw her
five best friends standing there.
She asked them to join her on
the balcony.

"Princess Celestia sent me to
Ponyville to study friendship,"
she began. "I didn't know very
much about that at first.

But now I know I wouldn't be here without my very best friends. I'm the luckiest pony in Equestria. Thank you friends, thank you everyone!"

As she stepped off the balcony everyone cheered.

Princess Twilight Sparkle had never felt so happy. She had a lot to learn about being a princess … but she knew that her best friends would be by her side!

The End

Well done!

You can continue your reading
adventures with the other
My Little Pony Early Readers:

Pinkie Pie's
Perfect Party

Rainbow
Dash's
Big Race

Applejack's
Sister Surprise